D0377752

AND OTHER ADVENTURE STORIES

Compiled by the Editors
of
Highlights for Children

Compilation copyright © 1995 by Highlights for Children, Inc.
Contents copyright by Highlights for Children, Inc.
Published by Highlights for Children, Inc.
P.O. Box 18201
Columbus, Ohio 43218-0201
Printed in the United States of America

All rights reserved

ISBN 0-87534-647-2

Highlights® is a registered trademark of Highlights for Children, Inc.

CONTENTS

By Marianne Mitchell

"Race you to the fort!" Adam shouted as he leaped over the low adobe fence. Jeff was close behind. The two boys sprang like jackrabbits across the desert toward a rocky outcrop behind Adam's house. They called it Fort Kerchoo because the sagebrush nearby made them sneeze.

"Watch out for dragons!" Jeff yelled, as tiny lizards skittered under rocks.

Soon they came to a dry wash that cut across the desert. "Now the brave explorers cross the raging river!" Adam said. He and Jeff marched across the sandy, dry arroyo. Next, they made a mad scramble for the top of Fort Kerchoo.

"I win!" Adam shouted, climbing onto the rock. "Let's look for coyotes or javelinas."

"I thought we were looking for gold," Jeff said.

"Yeah, gold!" Adam said. He slid off the rock and followed Jeff back to the wash. Any stone that sparkled in the sun was considered a valuable treasure. Fort Kerchoo already had a huge pile of glittery rocks. Some were studded with mica flakes. Others had chunks of pyrite that looked like real gold. "Fool's gold, for fools like us," Adam had said.

Adam liked walking the sandy bottom of the wash. Each rainstorm brought new surprises from the hills above. Once they found a flint arrowhead. Another time they picked up a sun-bleached cow skull. They called it their "dinosaur cow." Very rare.

"What's that over there?" Adam asked, pointing to a glassy chunk stuck in the dirt.

Jeff walked to where Adam was pointing and dug. In a moment he'd wiggled loose a large, transparent rock. "Wow! A quartz crystal!" Jeff said. He held it up to the sun. It was clear with tiny golden threads snaking through the center.

"Let me see," Adam said. Jeff handed him the rock, and Adam fingered the crystal as the sun danced off the sides. "This is the best rock we ever found!" he said.

"I saw a picture of this kind of quartz in our mineral book. I think it's called 'rutile quartz' because of the threads inside."

Adam handed Jeff the crystal, and he stuffed it into his pocket. "Let's see if we can find any more," Adam said.

Jeff headed down the wash, scuffing sand with his boot. Adam headed the other way. "Look out for dragons!" Adam shouted. Jeff smiled and kept on walking, studying the ground as he went.

After a while, Jeff climbed up on a big boulder and pulled the crystal from his pocket. He held it up to the sun, admiring its beauty. The sky overhead was as clear as the crystal, but dark clouds hugged the mountains to the west. He heard the rumble of thunder, and a sudden gust of wind was laced with the scent of distant rain. He stared at the cloudy mountain tops. Something about them bothered him.

A glint of light caught his attention, and he slid off the boulder to get a closer look. Down here, near the arroyo bottom, his ears picked up a strange sound. Was it a growl or a roar? Goosebumps ran up his arms. *It better not be a mountain lion,* Jeff thought. Where was Adam?

Jeff stood up, listening. The roar grew louder. Suddenly, the answer flashed in his head like lightning. He ran down the wash and found Adam poking in the sand.

"Let's get out of here, now!" he shouted.

"Why?" said Adam. "I want to look at . . ."

Jeff didn't let him finish. He grabbed Adam's arm and shoved him up the side of the wash. Then he scrambled up, grasping at prickly branches. In seconds, an angry, brown slush raced across the sand right underneath them. Small rocks tumbled through the water like toys.

"Look at that!" Adam gasped. "How did you know it was coming?"

"The noise," Jeff replied. "At first I thought it might be a lion or something. Then I remembered what Dad told me. It can be clear and dry here, but a storm in the mountains can send tons of water down the arroyos."

Jeff felt his pocket. The crystal was gone. In the rush to escape from the wash, he'd lost it. "It doesn't matter," he said. "Getting out was more important."

"Maybe the water will bring down real gold this time," Adam said as they watched the water roaring in the arroyo below them.

"Yeah. Fort Kerchoo could use some gold." Adam rubbed his nose. "Ah-ah-choo!"

Eagle-Eye Rescue

By Jerry Conley

Sarah Ryan peered through the binoculars and gasped. A car, parked next to the curb on a steep hill a few blocks away, had its front wheels turned in the wrong direction. When a car zoomed past, it rolled a few inches down the street.

Home with a cold, Sarah was looking over the city from the window of her family's high-rise apartment when she saw the car. The front wheels had caught Sarah's attention because she knew they should have been turned toward the curb.

"Come back!" she said helplessly, and stared again. As she watched, a huge truck went by and the old car moved. She wished her mother would hurry back from the drugstore.

As her mind raced to think of what to do, she saw another movement and looked closer. She gasped again—there was a child in the car!

Just then the faraway sound of a siren caught her attention. That's it. Call for help! She put the binoculars down, ran to the telephone, and dialed 911.

"This is 911," a voice said a moment later. "What is the nature of your emergency?

"Please, ma'am," Sarah said, "a little kid needs help." Sarah blurted out what she had seen.

"Take it easy," the woman said. "Let's go through it again. You can see a car over there, and it looks as if it's starting to slip downhill?"

"Yes, ma'am. That's right!"

"Where is it exactly?" the voice asked.

"I can't tell," Sarah said desperately. "It's three, maybe four blocks over. There are other buildings in the way, but I can see the top of the hill from here." She gave the woman her own address.

There was silence for a moment, then the woman said, "Don't hang up. I'll be right back."

It was quiet, then the woman came back on and said, "Can you take the phone over by the window?" Her voice was quiet and gentle, and she made Sarah feel better.

"Yes," Sarah said. "I'm by the window now."

"Good!" the woman replied. "Now look out and tell me when you see a helicopter."

Sarah looked, and at first she didn't see anything. Then she noticed a big helicopter whirling its way toward her. "I see it!" she said.

"Good! Now when he gets over your building, tell him which way to go."

Sarah gulped. "How?" she asked.

The woman chuckled, and it calmed Sarah a little. "You're connected to the pilot's radio," she said. "He can hear you."

"Loud and clear," another voice said.

In a few seconds the helicopter was right in front of her apartment window. "Over there," Sarah said as she pointed. "Over on the hill."

The big machine swung away. "This way?" the pilot asked.

"No. The other way!" Sarah shouted.

"Roger," the pilot said, and turned.

"There," Sarah yelled a minute later. "That's it. It's right down below you."

"Got it," the pilot said, and gave the woman the street names. "The kid is right," the pilot finished. "The car *is* rolling!"

The helicopter hovered. Sarah picked up the binoculars and tried to keep the phone from slipping, but it was hard. She took a deep breath as the station wagon moved a little faster. Then a police car pulled up. The danger was over.

"OK," the pilot said. "They got it." Then the woman came on again. "You still there?" she asked.

"Yes, ma'am," Sarah replied.

"You helped rescue that baby," the woman said. "You did a fine job!" She took Sarah's name and address, then hung up.

Sarah was still a little shaky when her mother walked in.

"You're better, aren't you?" she said, smiling. "Did you find something to do while I was gone?"

Sarah nodded her head. "I sure did, Mom," she said, grinning. "I definitely found something to do!"

ADRIFT

By David Lubar

They'd been in the raft for three days. Danny was pretty sure it was three days. He was afraid to ask—he didn't want to know if it had been longer. The days just blended together—drifting on an endless ocean, rocking gently on water they couldn't drink, floating under a sun they couldn't escape. It had started out so wonderfully. Danny thought back to the beginning of the trip.

"Let's go boys," his father had said as they got out of the car. Danny and his brother Mark grabbed the supplies from the trunk and walked along the dock to the boat. Gulls cried and circled above their heads as the dark green water lapped against the dock pilings below.

"Wow," Mark exclaimed as he got his first look at the boat they were borrowing. "Neat," Danny said. Then he stopped. "Dad, I left my book in the car." He put down the bag he was carrying and ran back to the parking lot.

"Come on!" Mark shouted. "Forget that stupid book. Just come on."

But Danny wanted his book. He opened the car door, reached into the back seat, and grabbed it. He liked that the small book felt much heavier than it looked. Obviously, this was a serious book. He glanced at the title—*The Audubon Field Guide to North American Fishes*. He'd gotten it last Christmas. It was the only thing he'd asked for.

"You really are crazy about fish," his father had said more than once. Danny knew his father didn't mind, though. Mr. Tennyson was a professor of history, and he was in favor of any kind of knowledge. Mark made fun of Danny's interest in fish, but what big brother didn't tease his younger brother once in a while?

Danny caught up and boarded the boat. He looked around. The boat belonged to one of the other teachers at his dad's college. The man was letting them use it for the weekend. They were going to cruise around, enjoy the weather, and maybe do a little bit of fishing.

It had all been so perfect, but it had gone horribly wrong. That evening something had happened to the engine and it caught fire. Terror filled Danny as he, Mark, and his father had tried to put out the fire. It got out of control so fast! They'd inflated the emergency raft, grabbed whatever food and water they could, and gotten away from the boat. In their panic, they had forgotten to take the emergency radio. No one knew they were adrift at sea.

They had drifted through the night. In the morning, they had no idea where they were. They took turns rowing east, hoping to find land.

When Danny wasn't rowing, he looked at his book. Sometimes he saw fish in the water. Once, a shark had come close to the raft. Another time, there'd been a school of mackerel.

"We're never going to get back," Mark said, breaking Danny's thoughts.

"Don't talk like that," Mr. Tennyson said. "We'll be fine."

"Yeah," Danny agreed. They still had food, and they had some water left. He knew everything would be OK.

But the day came and went. They finished the last of the fresh water. Danny felt very tired. He looked at his Dad and brother. They didn't have any energy either. He leaned against the side of the raft and dangled his hand in the water. Something flashed below. Danny looked. He was pretty sure he knew what it was. "A ladyfish," he said out loud, to no one in particular.

"Who cares?" Mark said. "You and your stupid fish," he muttered.

Danny didn't answer. Something important was trying to come through the fog in his brain. He found the fish in his book and tried to read the description. His eyes didn't want to focus. He blinked hard until things got less blurry, then he read the section. That was it! "Dad! Mark! I saw a ladyfish!"

His brother and father just looked at him.

"Don't you see?" Danny said. "They only live near shore. They don't go far from the shallows. We *have* to be near land. We just have to." He grabbed one of the oars and started paddling. Knowing that land was near, he found new energy inside himself.

His father joined him. When Danny got tired, he gave the oar to Mark. They took turns, paddling as hard as they could. Danny kept looking ahead, hoping, wishing, wanting to see land. In the water, he saw more ladyfish. But there was no land in sight. Then he saw other fish—small crevalle jacks, pinfish, and alligator gar. These were all fish that didn't venture far from the shore. Danny knew the raft had to be near the beach now.

"There!" Mark shouted, pointing ahead.

Danny squinted into the sun. Then he saw it too. "Land," he said, almost in a whisper. He reached down and clutched the book. It felt more solid than ever in his hand. He held it close as his father and brother paddled the last few yards to the beach.

Mark looked back at Danny. "I guess it is a good thing you had that book," he said, his voice hoarse from thirst.

"Yes," Danny said. "It is a good thing." He stepped onto the beach. Behind him, a million silver flashes streaked through the surf as the fish swam and leaped.

Treasure Tree

By P.C. Degenhart

An old fisherman was sitting on the wharf, whittling as he talked to Cara and Jeremy.

"After the ship was wrecked," he drawled as he pointed toward the ocean, "the three survivors took the chest of gold ashore."

"What did they do with it?" Cara asked excitedly.

"They carried it up into the redwood grove behind your house and buried it," the fisherman answered. "Then they rowed back to the wreck to get provisions. Just as they climbed on board the ship, a big wave rolled over, and all were drowned."

"Who got the gold?" Jeremy asked.

"Nobody," the old fisherman told him. "They buried it under the tallest redwood tree, and nobody's ever figured out which one it was."

"We could," Cara boasted, looking confidently at Jeremy.

"Yeah, let's try," he agreed.

Later, as the children were hurrying up the trail, Cara said, "If we could find the treasure, Dad wouldn't have to sell his redwoods to the logging company. He thinks these trees are wonderful."

"They are," Jeremy replied. "Some of them were growing here more than 2,000 years ago. Dad can use the gold to make the payment he's been worrying about, and we can save the trees."

"Let's hurry," Cara shouted, and dashed off into the grove.

"Maybe we should stick to the trail," Jeremy cautioned.

"If we stay on the trail, we'll never find the treasure," Cara answered.

So the children plunged into the tall ferns and dense underbrush and pushed their way along until they came to a huge log. Jeremy scrambled up onto it, then gave a hand to Cara. They could see more big trees, tall ferns, and a massive, ancient stump ahead.

"Let's climb on top of that big stump and look around," Jeremy said.

Together the children slid down off the log—and right on top of something black and soft that grunted, snarled, then went dashing off through the ferns and up the trunk of a tree.

"It's a bear cub!" Cara cried. "It must have been asleep by the log."

The cub stopped on a limb and whimpered.

"Let's run for the stump before the mother bear sees us," Jeremy said.

Just then they heard a crackling in the brush, and a fierce growl.

Jeremy grabbed Cara's hand and pulled her along through the ferns. In a few seconds they reached the stump, but the mother bear was right behind them.

Jeremy gave his sister a shove up the side of the stump. Cara caught at the rim and pulled herself up over the edge. Jeremy leaped for a bunch of salal brush that hung from the top and lifted himself up the side just as the mother bear reached the bottom of the stump.

She reared up. Cara picked up a stick that was lying on the stump and threw it toward the bear's nose. The bear angrily shook her head, opened her mouth, and roared.

Cara let out a terrified cry. Jeremy whirled just in time to see her disappear from sight. Then he realized they had been standing on a narrow rim—the middle of the huge stump was a deep, yawning hole.

"My leg's caught," Cara cried out. "I can't move."

Jeremy dropped down into the hole and crawled over to his sister. Her leg was wedged into a deep crack in the wood. He pulled gently on it, but Cara cried out in pain. "It hurts," she moaned.

"Take it easy, Cara," Jeremy told her. "As soon as the bear leaves, I'll go after Dad."

"She can smell us in here. She may never leave," Cara sobbed.

"If we're quiet, she may," Jeremy whispered.

The bear continued to circle the stump, growling and snarling. In the half-light it was terrifying. Cara began to cry. "Go get Dad. My leg. . ." Her voice trailed off.

"Cara," Jeremy cried in alarm. Cara's eyes were closed. Her face was white.

"I've got to get us out of here," Jeremy thought. He crawled up the steep side of the hole and peered over the edge. The bear was still pawing around the stump, sniffing and growling. How could he get past her?

Maybe he could fool her long enough to get away. He took off his jacket and threw it at her. She seized it in her paws and began to tear at it. Jeremy slipped down the other side of the stump and scurried through the ferns. He could hear angry growls. Was the bear tearing his jacket, or was she following him? He ran wildly without looking back.

He reached the trail, then gave a fearful backward glance. No bear. He tore down the trail and to the house in record time.

His father grabbed an ax and his stun gun, and they dashed back up the trail. They moved cautiously as they neared the stump, but the bear and cub had both disappeared.

His dad slid down into the hole and freed Cara's leg. Cara was still pale as Jeremy helped her up, but she was all right, just bruised and a little scared.

"Are you going to help us look for the treasure tree, Dad?" she asked.

"Do you mean to tell me that you fell for the old fisherman's tale?" her father laughed. "Hey, wait a minute!" he cried, and slid down the stump. "Look here, where the bear trampled down the ferns. The biggest burl I've ever seen."

What's a burl?" Jeremy asked.

"It's an abnormal growth on trees," explained his father, "sometimes on the trunk, sometimes on the exposed roots. It's very valuable, too, because it has a beautiful curly grain."

"But what's it used for?" Cara asked.

"Expensive wooden bowls and platters," answered their father as he pushed more ferns aside with his feet. "Furniture makers use if for an outside finish, a veneer. Kids," he added," this one is really a treasure. It'll bring a pretty price."

"Then we really did find a treasure tree!" Cara said, smiling.

By Marcella Fisher Anderson

Jake saw the shadow coming up the walk before he heard the knock. He shivered inside; people knocking at the front door always meant bad news. Not long ago, Reverend Gomes had knocked to tell him that his mother had died.

He watched now as his grandmother opened the screen door. Jake would always remember the flat sound of her voice.

"Jake," she said, opening the door for a tall, weather-beaten stranger. "This here's your father."

Jake stood motionless—like an egret watching fish. His father! After all these years?

Slowly, his father walked into the living room. "Sweet prophecies," he said looking at Jake. "How you've grown!"

Jake couldn't think of much to say to his father, nor could his father think of much to say to him. They talked very little—even on the long drive inland in his father's pickup truck. Jake just stared at the road as they journeyed away from Tampa and his grandmother's house to Lake Okeechobee and his father's wooden house.

One evening a few weeks later, after a supper of perch and corn cakes, Jake sat on the steps with his father. Not that he especially wanted to—there just wasn't much else to do. They didn't talk; the only sound was the lazy buzz of summer insects. Just then a turtle crawled out of the long shadow of the house.

Jake's father picked it up. "This here turtle has been around for some seventy-five years. He used to sit on a big rock in the stream out yonder. Your great-grandpappy carved his name and his birth date on that rock. Then your granddaddy carved his, too. Later, I carved my own. We were all boys about as old as you."

"Where's the rock now?" Jake asked.

"Covered with water," his father replied. "A few years ago, a flash flood made a new stream bed." Jake's father squinted his eyes at the turtle, then set it down on the sand.

"Will the turtle be back?" Jake asked.

"He'll be back. Just give him time."

Alone all day while his father worked, Jake ached for his mother. He missed his grandmother, too—she always knew when he was hurting and never thought he was too big to hold on her lap.

Finally, Jake decided he couldn't stand it any longer. One hot morning he packed some food in a paper bag and set out for Tampa. His grandmother would sure be happy to see him.

He followed a dry stream bed because he thought it might lead to Tampa Bay. He stopped at noon under a cottonwood tree and ate some biscuits. The dry, rustling leaves made him sleepy.

When he awoke, the sky was dark and Jake thought he'd better hurry on. Suddenly, rain came. When it pelted down harder, he walked with his head lowered. He didn't see the wall of water rushing down the dry stream bed, hurtling toward him. When he finally realized the danger, it was too late to climb up the bank.

Jake was caught in the churning torrent. He spun around, came up for air, and was dragged down again. Then he let himself be carried along, keeping his head above the water's surface.

Soon, up loomed the cottonwood where he had eaten lunch. He grabbed the lowest branch and swung himself along it, upside down, until he reached dry land. He stood up and looked around. Water squeezed between his toes on the wet sand as the cold rain continued to fall. In the distance, he saw the dull tin roof of his father's house.

Jake blinked. He had come back to where he had started; he hadn't gone anywhere after all.

It was getting toward evening. The rain finally slowed to a shower. His wet clothes felt chilly and clammy. With a sigh, he turned and started walking in the direction of the house, wading through new stream beds.

The wet, slippery porch rail was still warm from morning. He climbed the steps and turned around to watch the now-gentle rain. The rock was sticking up in a shallow stream, and Jake could see the carved names and dates. He stared at the muddy water swirling around the rock.

He hurried into the kitchen. He didn't know whether his father was home or not, and he wasn't certain he cared. He took a small knife from a drawer and waded to the rock. Silently, he worked on the stone surface.

When he was finished, he returned to the steps and sat down. From the corner of his eye, he noticed his father watching him from the doorway of the house. The man came out and sat down next to Jake.

"I won't ask you where you went or why you came back. It's enough to know you're here," he said. Jake said nothing.

"I was thinking," his father went on. "I could fix up your room and you could camp on the porch. Then your grandmother could come for a visit. Would you like that?"

The steps and rock swam before Jake's eyes. He barely heard what his father said next.

"I haven't been much of a father to you, son," he began. "I know that. I was always searching for the big money. When I couldn't make it, I was ashamed to come home to face you and your mother. She was a good woman, and I disappointed her."

Jake turned his head and really saw his father for the first time: the gray-blue eyes—so like his own—looking down at him. Jake spoke slowly, surprised at what he heard himself saying. "We look a little bit alike, don't you think? Maybe a little?"

His father's strong arm pulled him close, then he said, "Sweet prophecies! There's the rock. And you've put your own name and birth date on it!

You're some carver there, Jake. The only thing missing now is the turtle."

Jake felt a smile starting. A flow of warmth and happiness spread over his body. "Don't worry," he said. "He'll come around home again. Just give him time."

The Runaway

By Stephanie Moody

Chris and Old Paint had just crested a hill near the Broken Arrow Riding Stable when Chris heard the terrified screams.

"Help me! Help!"

In the distance Chris saw a big, white horse racing across the pasture. The horse's reins were flying loose, and the rider had slipped to one side.

Chris tightened her hands on Paint's saddle horn. She knew the rider and the horse—it was Jennifer, riding Dynamite.

Chris's mind whirled. Jennifer must have known better than to take Dynamite out of the corral. The mare was too spirited—she spooked at anything. Yet there they were, racing out of control across the meadow.

Chris trembled as Jennifer shouted again. No one else was in sight, and the panicked mare was heading for the barbed wire fence that enclosed the pasture.

Chris urged Paint down the hill. "Oh, why did Mr. Sanders make me ride you today?" she said. "You're too old and slow."

She nudged Paint into a lope, and they plowed through a tangle of bushes and trees. Branches smacked Chris's legs and stung her face and arms as Paint swerved to avoid the trees in their path. Chris shortened Paint's reins as they jumped a fast-running stream.

As Paint clambered up the bank, Chris could see Dynamite running just in front of them. Jennifer still clung to the saddle horn, her frantic screams echoing across the pasture. One of her legs was draped halfway over the saddle, and the stirrups were swinging wildly.

"Hold on!" Chris yelled, urging Paint to a gallop.

Chris leaned over the saddle horn as she and Paint moved up alongside Dynamite. Getting close to the frightened horse wouldn't be enough, she knew. They had to stop her. But how?

Dynamite's reins whipped just beyond Chris's reach, tempting her to grab them. She had seen riders stop horses that way on television, making a daring rescue. But what if she were to fall?

If only I could rope her, Chris thought, squinting her eyes to block out the dust. But even though Paint was used to a swirling rope from his days as a cow pony, Chris had never roped anything faster than a fence post.

Paint's breathing was labored as he raced closer to Dynamite. Paint was running as he had when he was younger, chasing a cattle stampede, trying to turn the cows back to safety.

"That's it!" shouted Chris. She nosed Paint next to Dynamite's withers. "It's our only chance. Turn her in circles, Paint. Turn her until she gets tired."

Chris shifted her weight, and Paint responded immediately. He edged closer to Dynamite. Chris gasped when she saw the barbed wire only yards ahead, its pointed strands threatening disaster. But she kept yelling encouragement to Paint.

She was turning the mare, just a little at first, then more and more. Paint finally nudged Dynamite away from the fence and kept turning her until they had made a loop. Around and around they went, slowing at last. Jennifer still clung to the saddle horn.

With a final snort, Dynamite stopped. Jennifer slipped to the ground.

"Jenny, are you all right?" Chris gasped, too weak to dismount.

Jennifer nodded. Mr. Sanders, the stable owner, had arrived in his truck.

"That was quick thinking," he called to Chris as he hurried over to Jennifer. "And mighty fine riding. Jennifer owes you a heap of thanks and I do, too. From now on, you can pick your own horse to ride. You've earned it."

Chris looked down at Old Paint, his sides still heaving from his run. "In that case," she said, stroking the horse's neck, "I'll pick Old Paint. I guess we make a pretty good team."

Old Paint pawed the ground. His friendly nicker seemed to say he had known it all along.

Storm at the Lighthouse

By Marjorie Belle Bishop

Tim was spending his vacation with Grandma and Grandpa Baker in Maine. He loved staying with them because they had the best job in the world—lighthouse keepers at Wolf Harbor. Tim had been here for short visits many times, but this time he would be here for the whole summer.

The lighthouse stood like a huge red-and-white-striped peppermint stick on a strip of land far out by the sea—a good mile from Grandma's and Grandpa's small white cottage. Each day Tim tagged along with Grandpa to and from the lighthouse. Every evening they turned on the light, and every morning they turned it off.

One afternoon when Tim went into the house to supper, he found his grandfather on the couch.

"My leg gave out, son. It's my arthritis kicking up again. You'll have to go to the lighthouse alone tonight. Think you can do that, Timmy boy?"

"Sure, Grandpa," Tim replied. "No problem."

"Just turn on the switch is all—and be sure to fasten the door. Eat your supper, boy, and then hurry. I won't rest easy till you're back," the old man said. Tim gulped down his food and scrambled into his jacket.

"Don't forget your flashlight," reminded Grandma, handing him Grandpa's big light.

It was still light outside, and Tim knew that if he hurried, he could be halfway back before it got dark. A fresh gust of wind kicked up little swirls of dust in the road. Soon he reached the lighthouse, but by then the sky had grown black. *There's a storm brewing,* he thought. *I'll have to hurry if I want to get home before it breaks.*

Tim hurried inside the lighthouse and turned the switch that sent the beacon shining out across the ocean. Thunderous-sounding waves were already tumbling and splashing over the rock wall that surrounded the lighthouse. Then the rain came—great torrents that beat against the lighthouse windows.

Tim paced back and forth in the small room. "I'm going to stay here until the storm is over," he decided aloud. He wasn't scared, but he would have felt better if Grandpa were here with him. Tim looked around the room. It was simply furnished with a stove, a couch, a table, and a broken chair. He was glad that Grandpa always kept the room fixed up in case of an emergency.

Some old magazines were stacked in a corner, and Tim sat down to look at them. The howling wind sent chills up and down his spine, and he couldn't sit still for long. He began to wonder if Grandma and Grandpa were worried. However, there wasn't anything Tim could do except stay here until the storm passed.

He climbed the ladder to the beacon. Somehow the bright, revolving lights were comforting. Tim's eyes followed the beacon as it shone far out over the angry, surging sea.

Suddenly the light fell on an object tossing crazily on the water. He waited for the light to flash back again. This time he riveted his eyes on the spot and, when the light returned, he saw a small dory with someone huddled in it!

The boat wasn't far from shore, but it was far enough to be in serious danger. Tim knew that the crashing waves would either capsize the boat or splinter it into pieces. He watched, half expecting the dory to disappear in the boiling waves.

At first the boat didn't seem to be making much headway toward shore, but all at once a series of huge waves pitched the dory toward the rocks. "What am I going to do!" Tim shouted. "I can't stand here and let the man drown!"

He clambered down the ladder and desperately looked around the room for anything he might use to help the man. Then he saw a coil of rope in the wood box. He grabbed the rope and his flashlight and raced out into the storm.

Guided by his flashlight, he picked his way among the rocks to the water's edge. At the same time he watched the light from the beacon for a glimpse of the dory. Had it been swept away? No, there it was, tossing and spinning in the wild sea.

Tim's mind raced with an idea. Quickly, he wrapped the rope around a large boulder. Tying it firmly, he then stood as close to the crashing waves as he dared and yelled, "Hey, there! Grab this rope!" He threw the rope as hard as he could toward the man. The man grasped the rope and held onto it frantically as Tim held on with all his might. The rope was cutting his hands, but he barely noticed.

The man tied the rope around his waist and jumped into the boiling sea. At that moment his tiny boat hit a rock and splintered with a crash. Tim held his breath, waiting for the man to surface. In a few seconds the man stood up in the shallow water and staggered forward.

"Are you all right, mister?" Tim asked anxiously.

The man nodded briefly. Tim took his arm and led him to the lighthouse.

"You saved my life, lad," the man murmured as he sank onto the couch. "The storm came up so fast, I didn't have time to get ashore."

The storm raged into the night. Tim warmed some soup for the man, who gulped hungrily, then fell into an exhausted sleep.

Tim must have slept, too, because the next thing he knew the door burst open and in came his grandfather with a group of people. Grandpa grabbed Tim in a huge bear hug as the others gathered around the man on the couch. Tim saw one man open a first-aid kit before Grandpa hugged him again. Sun streamed in from the open door.

"Timmy boy!" Grandpa said. "When the rescue team told me a boat had crashed in the storm last night, I was afraid it might have been you in the boat." A woman in a red jacket came over to Tim and his grandfather. She smiled and put her hand on Tim's shoulder. "If you hadn't been here, this man certainly would have died out there." The team helped the man walk out the door, and Tim and his grandfather followed.

Tim surveyed the wreckage on the beach. Scattered everywhere were huge clumps of seaweed, rocks, and debris covering the sand. In the middle of it all lay the battered remains of the dory. Grandpa locked the lighthouse door behind them, then took Tim's hand. "We'll go home and let your grandma feed us, then come back here and clean all this up," Grandpa said. Tim smiled up at his grandfather, and they trudged toward home.

Midnight Heroine

By Su Montour

Lightning ripped across the night sky, and thunderclaps shook the farmhouse windows where Kate Shelley sat watching the summer storm. Kate and her mother were the only people awake at the Shelley home that July night in 1881. Nearby, floodwaters of Iowa's Honey Creek and Des Moines River swirled dangerously beneath the railroad bridges that stretched over them.

Kate was fifteen. She loved the trains that passed by every day, and she knew their schedules by heart.

"The Midnight Express might be late tonight," Kate said to her mother. "Old Number 11 will probably be by." Number 11 was the "pusher" engine that helped trains up the steep curve near Kate's home. Sometimes it was sent out during storms to see if the tracks were safe before other locomotives were allowed through.

Kate was right. Number 11 chugged toward Kate's home, pushing through the storm to inspect the tracks. The engine slowed near the Honey Creek Bridge, and the section boss held his lantern high to see if the bridge was intact. The track and timbers seemed to be in place. He signaled to the engineer to continue. Number 11 rang its bell and lurched forward. Then came the terrible cracking of wooden beams as the weakened bridge collapsed under the engine's weight.

Back at their farmhouse, Kate and her mother jumped, startled by the sudden crash. A moment later they heard cries for help and the loud hiss of steam from the engine's hot boilers, which had plunged into the cold creek water.

Mrs. Shelley and Kate quickly fixed up an old railroad lantern, filling the oil cup and making a new wick from a piece of flannel. Mrs. Shelley lit the lantern and gave it to Kate, sending her off into the night.

Kate followed the cries for help. Past the shattered bridge timbers she spotted two men in the water clinging to large branches. Kate knew she wouldn't be able to save them alone.

It was then she remembered the Midnight Express. It would be carrying hundreds of passengers toward the broken bridge! To get help, Kate would have to cross the long Des Moines River railroad bridge to the nearest station.

Running hard, she reached the bridge and suddenly slipped and fell on the wet wooden ties. The lantern banged against the wood, and Kate heard the tinkle of broken glass as the lantern broke and went out.

The night suddenly became very black and frightening, but Kate did not stop. Rain and wind lashed her face as she crawled blindly from one slippery tie to the next. The spaces between the ties were wide—she could easily fall through and be swept into the swirling, muddy water far below.

But Kate knew she must not think of that now—she must get across. Lightning illuminated a large uprooted tree in the river that was barreling toward her. She froze in fear, imagining that the huge tree would destroy the bridge. But, at the last moment, the mammoth tree swerved and darted underneath, spraying her with mud and foam.

Kate clutched the rails and steadied herself, then continued on. Her skirt tore on the railroad spikes. Her hands and knees grew bloody and filled with splinters from the wood. She gritted her teeth and inched along for what seemed like hours.

Finally Kate felt the mud and cinders of the far bank under her. She scrambled to her feet and ran to the station. Breathless, she stumbled inside. The group of men inside were startled by the sight of the wet, white-faced girl who had burst through the door.

"Stop the Express!" she exclaimed. "Honey Creek Bridge is out!" Then, pale and exhausted, Kate slumped to the floor.

Unknown to Kate, the Midnight Express had already been stopped. But now, with help, Kate revived and told about the two survivors of Engine Number 11 trapped in Honey Creek.

An engine's whistle roused the villagers around the station. Volunteers with shovels and ropes boarded a nearby locomotive. Kate rode along and guided the rescuers down a path to the stranded brakeman and engineer.

Because of her heroic efforts, Kate was rewarded with a beautiful gold medal, a long gold chain, and a free train pass to last her lifetime. Trains even stopped at her house whenever she wanted to ride.

The old bridge that Kate crossed that stormy night is gone now. Today, the Chicago & Northwestern trains ride over the Des Moines River on a sturdy iron bridge. It's called the Kate Shelley Memorial High Bridge, named after the girl who risked her life to save the Midnight Express and the men of Engine Number 11.

A Stormy Friendship

By Maria Abissi

Frankie sweated as he turned the tractor's steering wheel. The whine of a small airplane in the distance sounded like a swarm of bees buzzing over his dad's cornfields. Frankie could see his sister Ana trudging toward him from the farmhouse. She was carrying a thermos that he knew was filled with cool lemonade. "Good!" Frankie said aloud. "Time for a break!"

He saw Ana look up, and then Frankie noticed the engine whine was louder than ever. He jumped from the tractor and saw a thick cloud of black smoke disappear behind a grove of trees to the south. *CRASH!* He heard trees snapping and breaking, and the cloud of smoke billowed over the trees.

"Who do you think it is?" Ana asked as she ran to Frankie. They both dashed toward the trees and peered through the brush. Twisted metal and broken plastic was everywhere, and in the middle of the wreckage was the cockpit and wings of a small two-seater plane.

Frankie recognized the wreck. The Johnsons had a plane like this one. Could Ben Johnson be trapped inside? Ana recognized the aircraft, too. "It's Ben!" she cried.

Frankie pulled at the door handle. "I can't get the door open," he gasped.

"Ben, are you okay?" Ana shouted. There was no answer.

Frankie and Ana looked at one another. Then without a word they raced back to the barn.

"Come quick, Dad!" Frankie yelled as he and Ana came up from the lower field. "He's hurt," Ana said, gasping for air.

"Who?" Dad asked.

"It's the plane from the Johnson's farm, and I think it's Ben," Frankie said.

Frankie had known Ben all his life, and he was a little jealous that Ben had his pilot license. Frankie didn't have his license yet; Dad thought he was too young to fly a twin-engine plane. Dad thought he was even too young to drive the tractor, but Frankie was able to convince him. Today was Frankie's first day plowing by himself.

"Ana, call Ben's father," said Dad. Ana disappeared inside the house.

"We better hurry, Dad," Frankie said. "A storm is coming." Frankie glanced toward the sky as he ran ahead of his dad. He remembered the time he was caught in a storm. Lightning crashed all around, and one of the horses was hit. Frankie could see the entire scene in his mind. He ran faster just as the first few raindrops hit.

As they approached, Frankie could hear someone calling. "That's Ben all right," Frankie called. He was relieved. Ben couldn't be hurt too badly if he was calling out for help.

"Ben?" said Frankie, anxiously trying to pry the door open again.

"Frankie, that you?" Ben said weakly. "My legs are stuck. I can't move."

"Don't try, Ben," Dad said. "Just hold on. We'll get you out." Thunder rumbled in the distance and Frankie's face tightened.

Ana raced down the hill yelling, "The phone lines are down, I couldn't get through! Is Ben in there? Is he okay?"

"His legs are caught," Frankie said, looking for another way to help his friend. "What if we used the truck to rip off the back of the plane?" Frankie asked his father.

"The plane might shift," Dad said, looking worried. "I guess we don't have any other choice, though." The storm was getting closer, and it began to drizzle harder.

"I can't feel my legs." Ben's voice was faint.

"Let's do it Dad! What choice do we have?" Panic filled Frankie's voice.

"Frankie and Ana, you stay with Ben. I'll get the truck." The thunder rolled louder, and it began to rain harder.

Frankie climbed onto the plane and looked through the windshield. He could see his friend trapped inside. Ana huddled beside the door, talking to Ben. "Everything's gonna be okay, just hang on," she said as cheerfully as she could. Frankie could see Ben was in pain.

Ben seemed to sense Frankie's and Ana's nervousness, and he tried to smile. Frankie slid off the plane and joined Ana at the door. They began talking to Ben about all those long summer days swimming and fishing. They talked to Ben for what seemed like hours.

"What happened to Dad?" Frankie finally asked Ana. She shrugged her shoulders.

I don't think Ben can wait any longer," Frankie said. "We better use the tractor." It was still in the field where Frankie left it. He hesitated for a moment, thinking about all the arguments he and Dad had about the tractor. Then he raced to the big machine and carefully drove it through the now-muddy fields toward the wreck.

"Help me hitch it to the back," he said to Ana when he returned. "Tie it to the rudder," he shouted. It was raining so hard they could hardly hear each other.

Once Ana had it secure, she gave the signal. The noise was unbelievable—the tractor roaring, wheels spinnning, rain pounding, the plane rocking. The cracking noise as the plane pulled apart was deafening. Then, *SNAP!* Frankie scrambled to the front of the plane, just as Dad walked toward them.

"The truck got stuck in the mud," Dad said. "You did the right thing by using the tractor. Now let's get Ben to safety."

Dad helped Frankie pull Ben from the wreckage. Ben's body looked limp. Lightening flashed in the sky.

A couple of days later Frankie was jolted awakc by thunder. He could hear Ana talking, "Why, Ben Johnson, you're soaked to the bone. Why on earth would you come out, in your condition, on a day like today?"

Frankie sprang up from the couch and ran to the kitchen. There, standing at the door, was his best friend—on crutches with one leg in a cast.

"Only one leg is broken," Ben exclaimed, "the other's just bruised real bad."

"We were worried about you," Ana said.

"The reason I came over was to thank everyone for what you did." Ben looked at Frankie.

Frankie grinned. "I'm just glad you're okay, buddy."

"I couldn't have made it without you, Frankie. You're a real friend," Ben said clapping Frankie on the back.

Outside, lightning danced around the house, but Frankie paid no attention. They had a friendship that could weather any storm.

By Nancy T. Galloway

"Aw, Mom," Tracy said throwing the first-aid manual on the floor, "why do I have to study this dumb stuff? And on Saturday, too. I want to go bike riding with Karen and David."

"It's not 'dumb stuff.' It's important," Mrs. Conners said. "If you're going to take care of Lori Thatcher afternoons after school, I want you to know what to do in an emergency."

"If anything happens, I'll call you."

"What if I'm not home?"

"I'll call 911. I don't need to know any of that first-aid junk."

"It's good to call 911, but you need to know what to do while you're waiting for help to arrive," Mrs. Conners said.

"But Karen, David, and I were going to have a picnic in the park today," Tracy said.

Mrs. Conners looked at her watch. "It's early yet. If you study for an hour, I'll pack a lunch for you to take to the park. You'll have plenty of time to have some fun and still be back before dark. Now get busy," she said.

"All right," Tracy said with a sigh. She picked the book up and settled down to read. An hour passed quickly. Soon Mrs. Conners was back.

"Time's up. Karen and David are waiting out front," she said, handing Tracy a bulging backpack. "There's peanut butter and jelly sandwiches, apples, a thermos of milk, and chocolate chip cookies in here. Have a good time."

"Thanks, Mom," Tracy said. "See you later."

"Be careful," Mrs. Connors said, "And don't forget to be home before dark."

Karen and David were waiting outside with their bikes.

"Hurry up!" David shouted.

"If we don't hurry," Karen said, "my bratty little

brother will show up and want to come with us."

"Too late," David said. "Here comes Brian now."

Brian was pedaling his bicycle as fast as he could toward Tracy's house. "Wait for me!" he yelled.

Tracy groaned, and Karen cupped her hands around her mouth and yelled, "Go back home. You can't come with us."

"Mom said I could go with you," Brian panted as he pulled up in the yard.

"You won't be able to keep up," Karen said.

"Sure I will," Brian insisted.

"Aw, let him come," David said.

"Yeah, we might as well let him come," Tracy said. "We've got plenty of food. If we don't take him, he'll just follow behind us anyway."

"All right," Karen said. She glared at Brian and added, "But you'd better keep up."

Tracy strapped on the backpack, and the four of them took off for the park. After hiking around the lake, they played catch with a Frisbee David had brought along. Later, they sat under the trees and ate their picnic lunch. When they were finished, they fed scraps to the ducks and put the trash in the recycling bins. It was late when they started for home.

"We've got to hurry," Tracy said. "I'm supposed to be home before dark."

"Me, too," Karen said.

"Why don't we take the shortcut through Baker's Woods," David suggested.

"I don't know," Tracy said. "It's kind of rough riding. What about Brian?"

"I'm no baby. I can ride just as good as you can," Brian insisted.

"Oh, he'll be all right," Karen said. "Let's go."

It was almost dark when they reached Baker's Woods. Tracy, Karen, and David stopped on the far side of a ditch to wait for Brian. Brian was pedaling hard when suddenly his bike hit a half-buried log. He went flying through the air and landed face down in the ditch. He didn't move. For a long moment, no one moved.

"Somebody do something," Tracy yelled, but David leaned against a tree looking as if he might be sick, and Karen dropped her bike on the ground and began to cry. Tracy wanted to cry, too, or run away, but someone had to help Brian. She forced herself to think, to try to remember what she had read just this morning.

"David, give me your jacket," she ordered. "Then ride to the main road. Stop the first car you can and ask whoever's driving to call 911."

David tossed his jacket to Tracy and took off. Tracy knelt beside Brian and put her hand gently on his back. He was breathing regularly. Blood ran down his face from a cut on the side of his head, and his face was very pale. She put David's jacket over Brian's shoulders and covered his legs with her jacket. Next she brushed the dirt and weeds away from his face.

"Karen," Tracy said, "stop crying and give me your bandanna."

Karen untied the bandanna from a belt loop on her jeans and handed it to Tracy. "Is he dead?" she asked fearfully.

"No, just hurt." Tracy folded the bandanna and placed it against the cut on Brian's head, pressing down firmly.

Brian's eyes flickered open. "Oh," he said. "My head hurts awful."

"Lie still Brian," Tracy said. "You're going to be OK, but you have to be still so I can hold this cloth on your cut."

It seemed like a long time before the ambulance arrived. Her arms ached and her legs had gone to sleep from being in one position for so long.

"Good work," the paramedic said to Tracy. "Brian's going to be all right, thanks to your quick thinking. It's a good thing you knew what to do."

"You can thank my mom and the first-aid manual for that," Tracy grinned.

AVALANCHE!

By Ann Jensen Devendorf

Sam felt the warm, dry Chinook wind on his face as he hurried from the corral to the ranch house. Once inside the house, Sam wrote a note to his mom and put it on the refrigerator where she would find it when she came back from town. It read: *I am going to ski Buck Mountain.*

Sam knew it was dangerous to ski when the Chinook was blowing, but he couldn't resist one last, fast run before spring came to the mountains.

Putting on his boots and skis and grabbing his

poles, Sam skied up the mountain with long, gliding steps. When the mountain became steep, he used the herringbone step, leaving a long line of tracks. As the angle of the mountain became almost straight up and down, he sidestepped to reach the top.

At the top he rested. Then he jammed his cowboy hat down on his head, pulling a loop of cord under his chin. Pushing hard with his poles, he dropped downward with the speed of a diving eagle. Turning on the mountain with a rooster-tail spray of snow, he traversed the face of it. Turning again, he started another downward drop.

From behind came a roar. Sam glanced over his shoulder. A huge wall of snow—uprooting trees and rolling boulders as if they were marbles—sped toward him.

Sam turned and frantically tried to outrun the avalanche, but it was useless. The snow caught him and tumbled him over and over. *I did a triple somersault,* he thought in amazement. He shot down the mountain in a maelstrom of snow. After long minutes, he came to a stop.

He pushed the snow from his eyelids, nose, and mouth. He lay in darkness. *I can breathe,* he thought. *There's air.* He moved his legs and was glad he could do so. He murmured a thanks for the safety bindings that had released his skis.

Sam tried to raise himself out of the snow, but he couldn't. Whenever he struggled for footing, he sank further into the snow. There seemed no bottom to it. Sam began to panic. *I must not panic,* he said to himself. *Dad always says never panic.*

Sam lay quietly spread-eagled in the snow, thinking *Mom will have seen my note. Mom and Dad will have heard the avalanche. They'll call the ski patrol and come looking for me.*

Sam's head felt cold. He realized he'd lost his hat. "I hope it's lying on top of the snow right over me," he said aloud. "That way they can find me." He ran the comforting thought around in his mind, but then realized it wasn't very likely.

Sam's hands felt cold. "Wish I'd worn gloves," he whispered. He put his right hand into the pocket of his jacket and felt his scarf. It was a red scarf, he knew. *I wish I could get that scarf to the top of the snow over me,* he thought. *It would bring the searchers to me. I need a stick, a long stick. I wonder if one of my ski poles is near.*

Moving his arms slowly and carefully, Sam searched the snow around him. His fingertips found the metal of a ski pole. He drew it toward him. He stuck the scarf on the point of the pole and pushed the pole upward as far as he was able. After that, he wiggled his toes and fingers to keep them warm. He lay quietly saying to himself over and over, *don't panic.* It seemed a long while before he heard voices. He tried to shout but his voice, muffled by snow, seemed useless.

The voices were right over him! Seconds later, Sam saw the light of day, as the snow was shoveled and pushed from him. He was lifted from the snow by Dad and a member of the ski patrol. His Mom hugged him and brushed the snow from his hair. The ski patrol wrapped Sam in blankets and strapped him to their rescue toboggan for the trip back to the ranch house.

"If it hadn't been for that scarf sticking out of the snow, I doubt if we would have found you," said Dad. "I'm happier than you'll ever know that you didn't panic."

"I kept my cool," said Sam, trying to make a small joke.

Mora and the Monsoon

By Bernadine Beatie

Mora threw a last handful of grain to the chickens and smiled as she watched them scratch contentedly in the earth. Then she glanced toward the cooking shed where her grandmother had gone to make *chappatis* (the flat pancakelike bread of India). The door to the shed was closed, so Mora skipped across the yard. She sat down, brushed the ground clean, and drew the letters her ten-year-old brother Gulab had taught her. She tilted her head to one side and printed her own name.

"M-o-r-a—Mora," she whispered softly. Then she printed the letters p-i-t-a. "*Pita*—father," she said. Mora did not remember her father or her mother. They had died years ago when the river flooded. Now a dam had been built many miles up the river, and the danger of floods was gone.

"Mora," her grandmother called from the door of the cooking shed.

Quick as a flash Mora erased the words and letters, but Grandmother had seen. "You should not waste your time with letters," she said crossly. "There are more important things for a girl to learn."

"Gulab says that many girls in India go to school now," Mora said.

Grandmother frowned. "I did not go to school," she said. I learned all of the things I needed to know in the home of my mother and my grandmother, just as you must learn."

"You have already taught me to cook and sew, Grandmother," Mora said. "If only you would let me go to school with Gulab, I would rise at dawn each day to do my share of the work."

Grandmother answered, "And still walk six miles to school and six miles back home as Gulab does? No, Mora, schooling is not for a girl."

Mora turned away. Her heart was heavy. Each day she watched longingly as her older brother and three other boys from their village started the long walk to the nearest school, located in a larger village to the south. Then she either helped her grandmother in the house or worked in the fields with her grandfather.

Each day Grandfather looked at the sky, hoping for rain. But the sky stayed clear and bright. The earth in the fields cracked and split, and the grain turned brown.

"If the rains do not come soon," Grandfather said, "there will be hunger in the village this year."

In spite of her grandfather's great worry, Mora was happy. Her brother Gulab was helping her learn to read. Each night he printed new words on his slate. Mora learned them and begged for more. Gulab could barely keep up with her. Grandmother grumbled but did not forbid the teaching.

"You learn quickly, Mora," Gulab said one night. "I can't teach you much more. You can read. You should go to school and become a teacher."

"Teacher, indeed!" Grandmother exclaimed. "Can a teacher cook better food than I can?"

"No one cooks better food than you, Grandmother," Gulab said. His eyes twinkled as he continued. "My teacher often speaks of another food you can't cook. He says that books are food for the brain. Mora needs that food, too."

"Humph!" said Grandmother. "If it does not rain soon, you will find that it is rice, not books, that fills your belly."

That night the rains started. The next morning Mora helped Grandmother pack clothes for Gulab. He and his friends would stay with the schoolmaster until the monsoon was over. Mora was sad as she stood at the door waving good-bye to her brother. She would learn nothing new until the rains were over.

Day after day the rains continued. The river rose and covered the roads. Soon the village was cut off from the outside world. The elders of the village shook their heads, remembering other floods. They were thankful for the great dam. Without it, their crops would have been washed away, and they would have had to leave their homes and go to the safety of the hills.

Rain poured from a leaden sky. There was only one radio in the village, and each morning Mora and her grandfather went to the market at the edge of town to hear the news. Every day the news was bad. Streams and rivers all over the country were flooding. Many people had been forced to leave their homes.

Finally, the rains stopped, but the river rose and the skies stayed dark and threatening.

Early one morning Mora heard a loud humming in the sky. She ran outside, followed by her grandmother and grandfather. All the villagers ran from their homes, chattering and pointing to the sky. An airplane circled overhead, and then flew lower and lower. Finally, a man leaned out and dropped a small box. He waved, and the plane zoomed up and away like a great bird.

The elders opened the box. Inside was a piece of paper with a message written on it. They looked at each other. No one could read it, and the village letter-writer had left long before the monsoon had started.

Mora ran to her grandfather. "I can read the message," she whispered shyly.

The men laughed and the women of the village looked at each other, shocked that Mora should be so bold. They were sure that this young girl could not read.

But just then Mora's grandmother walked up and stood beside her. "Read the message, Mora," she said. Then turning to the women, she remarked proudly, "Mora can read."

Mora spelled out the letters into words. Her face paled. "There is a crack in the dam!" she cried. "They are afraid it will break. We must flee to higher ground."

The villagers ran to their homes, loaded their most precious possessions into small carts, and fled to the hills. There they built crude shelters and waited for news of the dam.

The next morning the plane came again. It circled the hills until the villagers were found. Another message was dropped, along with food and clothing. This time the elders did not laugh when Grandfather took the note to Mora. The women and children gathered about her excitedly.

Mora's face brightened as she read. "The dam is holding," she explained, "but we must stay here a few days longer. They will come again and let us know when it is safe to return to our homes."

"Who would have thought," said one of the women, "that we could learn so much from a small piece of paper." She turned to Mora's grandmother. "I have taught my daughter only how to sew and to prepare food. She should learn to read like Mora."

Mora was pleased, but also a bit frightened. She looked at her grandmother in surprise. She could hardly believe her eyes, for her grandmother, who was usually so serious, looked straight at her and closed one eye in a wink. Then she stood up very straight and said, "There is food for the brain as well as for the belly. My Mora will go to school with Gulab. She will be a teacher. Perhaps someday she will teach the children of our own village. Then all will read. Is that not so, Mora?"

"Yes, Grandmother! Oh, yes!" Mora's smile was almost as bright as the sun that just then burst through the dark clouds above them.

INCIDENT ON THE BRIDGE

By Neil C. Fitzgerald

"Watch out for my line!" Ricky called.

"I see it!" Erin shouted back.

They stood on the bank, watching the canal current move swiftly. They could hear the pounding surf of the bay at the end of the canal. The day was cold, but the bluefish were running. Nothing compared to hauling a blue from the canal.

Erin saw the boat first. "Ricky, look!"

A dinghy with a sail bobbed in the current, heading for the open water. *Has to be a tourist,*

Ricky thought. *No native would be dumb enough to sail such a flimsy boat on a day like this.*

Erin set down her pole. "It's just a kid," she said. "And he's in trouble!"

Ricky watched the boat swirling in the current. "He's lost control. He needs help!" Ricky scanned the shores of the canal. A pair of cormorants watched from an old dock. A lone gull circled above. But no other people were in sight.

The boy in the boat had spotted Erin and Ricky and yelled for help. Erin heard the fear in the boy's voice. "Stay calm!" she shouted.

What could they do? Swimming was out. Even on the calmest days the current was treacherous.

Ricky grabbed his tackle box and took out his knife. He quickly cut the hooks from his line. "We need to find the heaviest sinker in the box."

Erin rattled through the box and pulled out a sinker. Ricky tied it to the end of his line. "I see!" Erin exclaimed. "You're going to cast the sinker into the boat and then pull him to shore."

Erin looked down at the big rocks that formed the bank of the canal. "His boat will be smashed," she said.

"It's the only way we can save him!" Ricky yelled.

Erin nodded, then ran to her bike. "I'm going for help," she said.

Erin raced away. The dinghy was closer to Ricky now. He raised his pole, put it behind him, and heaved. The sinker flew through the air and splashed into the water a few feet from the boat.

The boy saw what Ricky was trying to do. Next time he would be ready. Ricky reeled in as fast as he could, reared back, and sent the sinker flying again. The boy leaned forward, but the sinker slipped just short of his outstretched fingers. "Take your time," Ricky said to himself.

He reeled in again, then hurled the sinker skyward. It soared out over the canal, but the current had carried the boat farther from the bank. The sinker fell short again. The current was sweeping the boy and his boat away from him. Ricky saw one last glimmer of hope. The railroad bridge!

Pole in hand, he hopped onto his bike and pedaled furiously. He reached the bridge and looked back for the dinghy. There was still time.

A thousand times his mother had warned him, "Keep off the railroad bridge. It's no place for children to play." Ricky pushed the thought away and climbed onto the bridge. He raced to the middle and laid down flat.

The dinghy spun toward the bridge. Ricky lowered the sinker until it dangled a few feet above the water. The boy knew what to do.

One chance to connect. Ricky lay still, waiting. Then he felt vibrations in the track and looked up. The white light of the train was approaching. There was just time enough to get up and run. Ricky looked at the boy, then at the train.

Ricky shoved the fishing pole between his legs, rolled to the edge of the bridge, and grasped the sides. He swung onto a girder below as the train sped onto the span. The bridge shook, and Ricky's heart pounded. He held his breath. As he peered at the churning water below, the giant shadow of the roaring train engulfed him.

Quickly the train sped away. Ricky struggled to right himself. The boy was almost directly below him. Ricky lined up the sinker. The boy lunged and caught it.

Ricky jammed the pole between the tracks and grasped the line. It cut into his hands as the current fought to pull the boat and the boy from his grasp. Then from the distance Ricky heard the sweet sound of sirens racing toward him. "Oh, thank you, Erin," he whispered and fought to hold on.

Moments later they were there—fire fighters, police officers, and Erin. The fire fighters worked quickly, and soon everyone was hugging the boy and Ricky.

Later, as Ricky started home on his bike with

Erin beside him, he looked across the canal. Everything was quiet as before. The gull had disappeared, but the two cormorants still sat watching from the dock.

Ricky shook his head and looked at Erin. "Come on," he said. "I'll race you home."

By Linda Oatman High

By the light of a full moon and a half-empty oil lamp, Sadie Stoltzfus heaved a sigh as she slopped the pigs, collected some eggs, and gave Aarie an apple and a big handful of oats. Aarie needed extra nourishment, for soon she would give birth to a new foal.

Across the dusky barn, Sadie's brother Sam was busy milking the cows. "Give Aarie more hay, Sadie," he shouted through the stalls. "She needs a warm bed tonight."

The sky was thick with smoky black storm clouds, and the wind seemed to bite at Sadie's and Sam's faces as they walked through the barnyard toward the farmhouse. Even though they both wore heavy wool coats, Sadie and Sam were shivering in the cold. Snowflakes were falling so fast they stung Sadie's nose, and the frost-frozen ground was covered with a white snow blanket that looked like fresh white milk.

"I'll bet we'll get a blizzard tonight," Sam said. He packed a snowball and threw it at the barn. Neither of them noticed that the door to the barn stood open, creaking slightly in the bitter wind.

"May we go out sledding after supper, Dad?" Sam asked, looking across the table at his father, who was ladling steaming chicken soup into bowls.

Mr. Stoltzfus smiled at his children and his blue eyes lit up like a summer sky. "Yes . . . I suppose so. Just be careful. It's a bone-chilling, frost-biting, tooth ch-ch-chattering winter's night."

Sadie and Sam giggled at their father. He could brighten up the darkest winter night.

An hour later, Sadie and Sam were skimming down Cowpath Hill like greased pigs. At the bottom of the steep hill was a tiny creek. Across the creek was a sharp drop that disappeared down the side of Welsh Mountain. "You'd fall right off the edge of the earth if you tried to sled down that mountain," Sam said as they dug their boots into the snow so they wouldn't land in the stream.

The snowstorm had become even more fierce, and the wind sounded like a train whistle as it whipped through the trees. Sadie could hardly see her brother through the frenzied flakes blowing in every direction. It reminded her of a water globe, the kind you shake to see the snow flurry.

"Well, Sam, you were right," Sadie said as they trudged slowly up the hill, pulling their sleds. "We got a blizzard, all right."

As they neared the top of the hill, Sadie and Sam were out of breath and the cold was squeezing their lungs. "Whew!" Sam collapsed on his sled and breathed deeply, blowing cold clouds of breath steam before his face.

Suddenly, a dark form shot by. Sadie shrieked, "It's Aarie! She's out of the barn!"

They could barely see the horse through the snow. Her swollen belly swayed as she plunged down the hill. Sadie and Sam stared as Aarie reached the bottom of the incline and leaped across the stream. "She's gone crazy," Sam whispered.

"Well, don't just stand there!" Sadie's voice seemed to cut through the snow like a knife. "We have to go after her." Sadie jumped on her sled and pushed off. Snow pelted her face and she could hear the old wood of Sam's sled squeaking beneath his weight as he followed right behind.

When they reached the creek, Sadie and Sam hopped from rock to rock, lugging their sleds. When they got to the other side of the stream, they stumbled to the edge of the Welsh Mountain and looked down into the darkness. Aarie was nowhere in sight. "The edge of the earth," Sam whispered, as they prepared to sled into the unknown.

They plummeted down . . . down . . . down, steering away from rocks and trees, holding their breath as they plunged into the frosty darkness. It was like falling into a bottomless pit or being on a roller coaster that never ends.

Finally, they reached the bottom and stopped their sleds with a jolt at the edge of a huge frozen lake. "This must be Icedale Lake," Sadie said. "Dad used to skate here when he was a boy."

Sam tested the ice and found that it was frozen solid, with several inches of snow on top. Suddenly, from somewhere on the lake, they heard a faint whinny. Aarie! Sadie and Sam began to slide and run across the ice and then, in the milky light of the white snow, they saw her.

Aarie was on her side, gently nudging a wobbly-legged colt into a standing position. There, on the ice, with snow falling all around him, the little white-faced foal took his first steps.

"Hi, Mama," Sam said to Aarie, rubbing her velvety nose. Aarie almost seemed to smile.

"He's beautiful, Aarie," Sadie said. "What shall we name him?"

"Blizzard." Sam's voice was as soft as the fallen snow. "We'll call you 'Blizzard,' little white-face."

They trudged back up the steep hill toward the farmhouse as the snowstorm abated. The Man in the Moon smiled down at them, and soft snowflakes melted on their faces. Their feet were cold and their hands were cold, but ahead of them, Sadie and Sam saw the warm lights of home.

THE SCOUT

By Darlene Goff Dobson

Little Hawk moved cautiously along the moon-lit trail. Alone in a strange place, he relied upon all his senses. Sniffing the air, he knew neither grizzly nor rattler was near. But damp, earthy smells and bubbling sounds told him the spring was close by.

When a dry twig snapped beneath his moccasin, he froze. Somewhere nearby a coyote howled. The eyes of those prowling the night were now upon him. Yet he knew he must go on; to turn back would make him a coward.

Thinking only brave thoughts, he continued. His ears guided him safely to the stream. Quietly, he filled the water pouch and began to retrace his steps to his small camp.

Little Hawk had grown up listening wide-eyed to the tales of dangerous adventures told by the scouts of his Oglala village. But it was the stories told by his grandfather—the greatest Oglala scout—that excited him the most. He wanted nothing more than to be a scout. Although he had spoken of this desire to no one, Grandfather knew.

Many times the two traveled together, Grandfather patiently teaching him the ways of a scout. However, this time things were different. Never before had Grandfather insisted that he go alone or taken him this far from the Oglala village.

A deep prairie stillness settled in around him as he wrapped himself in a blanket and settled near his campfire. Tears threatened to spill. "I will not shame myself," he said. "Surely Grandfather will return before sunrise."

It was midday when Little Hawk awoke. Quickly he looked around, hoping to find Grandfather. Instead he saw the water pouch lying empty at his side. "A fine scout you are," he muttered. "Someone enters camp and pours your water on the ground and still you sleep."

Rising, he jogged to the spring. "Where do I go from here?" he said. "Will I find my people or the enemy?" Squatting to fill the water pouch, he spied moccasin prints in the soft mud. He studied them carefully. They were blurred, almost as if someone had tried to erase them. Little Hawk rose. Now he would become a tracker.

He moved from the spring bank to the open areas and glided through the tall prairie grasses, searching the horizon for danger. Now and then he stopped and scanned the landscape. Nothing escaped his piercing glance. No movement or sound went unnoticed.

Suddenly, Little Hawk gave a leap of joy. In the distance, rising out of the plain, stood the Black Hills! His people made their summer camp near the mountains. When next the sun goes down, his heart sang, I will be safe in the lodge of my father.

He sensed a slight movement behind him. Though he saw or heard nothing, he knew someone followed. The words of the old scout echoed in his ears: "A tracker should always remember that perhaps someone also tracks him."

Not once did he catch a glimpse of his stalker, not even a shadow. *This one knows the way of the wolf,* he thought, as he moved swiftly but warily along.

The day ended and the moon grew big and round. Little Hawk kept moving. No matter how exhausted he was, he dared not stop. Hunger gnawed at his stomach. His legs ached. How he longed to feel his horse under him, to ride away from danger. *If I cannot outrun this enemy, then I must outsmart it,* he told himself. *Let surprise be on my side.*

For hours he circled and double-backed his path. Finally, in the gray half-light of dawn, he spotted a movement on the trail behind him. Little Hawk's eyes focused on a large boulder. Climbing on top, he flattened himself against the cool surface. Through quivering lips he whispered to Wakan-tanka, the Great Mystery, "Make me brave and strong."

Scarcely breathing, he watched the enemy pass below. Then with a loud whoop he plunged downward. He struck the man a hard blow across the back and both scouts tumbled to the ground. Little Hawk immediately sprang to his feet. "Grandfather, it's you!" he cried. "Are you hurt?"

The old scout glanced up, and a slow smile parted his lips. "No, Grandson."

Little Hawk took Grandfather's hand, helping him to stand. "The tracks by the spring were yours. You emptied my water pouch," he said.

"Yes, I tested you. Now I have much praise for a young one so cunning and brave. When our people call upon you, you will be ready." The old scout's eyes sparkled. "My grandson, the Oglala scout."

With those words Little Hawk's heart took wings, soaring until he felt it touch the stars. "Little Hawk, the Oglala scout."

The Storm

By Karen Hayes Murray

"Mom and Dad won't be able to get back, will they?" Jesse asked.

Carol didn't answer her little brother right away. Even without the binoculars, she could see the waves washing over the causeway that connected their island to the mainland half a mile away. "Well, not for a while," she said. "Not until the tide is lower."

"That means we'll be alone until after bedtime," Jesse said. His voice trembled. "What if something happens? What if the water comes right up to the house, or the wind blows it down?"

Carol had thought about those things, too. The storm had arrived much faster than anyone expected. Wind drove the rain against the house, and the bay was a boiling mass of waves. But she couldn't let Jesse be frightened.

"It won't blow down. Think how old this house is, and how many hurricanes it's been through." She had an idea. "Let's make believe that we're in a fort, and we're surrounded by the enemy."

Jesse's face lit up. He was always building forts for his toy soldiers. "And we have to hold out until the relief force arrives. What's our strategy?"

"You get the emergency supplies, in case the power goes out. I'll strengthen our fortifications."

Jesse ran into the storeroom and came out with a flashlight, an oil lamp, and a radio.

Carol grinned. Her idea was working. She got a roll of masking tape and taped long strips like a tick-tack-toe board across the picture windows. That would help keep the glass from shattering if the windows broke from the wind. Now if only she could keep Jesse calm until their parents returned.

The phone rang. Carol jumped up to answer it, and Jesse ran into the kitchen to pick up the other phone. There was a burst of static, then her father's voice: ". . . hear me, Carol? Harbor Bridge is washed out . . . try to take Beach Road. We'll be home as soon as . . ."

"Dad, the causeway is washed out," Carol shouted. "You can't get here by car."

"What? The causeway? I can't hear you, Carol. Are you and Jesse all right?"

Everything's fine here," Carol yelled. "Don't worry, Dad. Stay where it's safe." There was so much static that she wasn't sure her father understood.

His voice came faintly through the static: "Cormorant Point . . . boat from there . . ." Then the phone went dead. At the same instant the lights went out.

Jesse ran to the window. "Look, a telephone pole on the causeway fell down!"

Carol stared out into the storm. The three poles near the house still stood, but the fourth was gone, and the wires went down into the waves.

Jesse looked frightened. Carol took his hand. "Light the emergency lamps, Captain. The enemy has cut off our communications."

"What did Dad mean about a boat from Cormorant Point?" Jesse asked as he turned on the flashlight and handed Carol the oil lamp.

"Maybe they're going to take a boat from the rescue station," Carol said as she lit the lamp.

Jesse went to the window facing the Point. "The waves are much bigger than whitecaps," he said.

Carol took a look through the binoculars. Cormorant Point was a quarter mile across the mouth of the bay. She could see the lighted windows of the rescue station, but everything in between was boiling white. The thought of her parents trying to cross the bay in a boat was terrifying.

"Jesse, we have to send a message somehow," Carol said.

"Why don't we do Morse code in the window with the flashlight?" Jamie said. "Dots and dashes for SOS."

"We don't want to say SOS," Carol said. "That means *help!*"

"Yeah," Jesse said. He frowned. "But those are the only letters I know."

"Letters . . . ," Carol said. "I've got it!" She grabbed the masking tape and began taping wide lines on the glass.

"Wow! Do you think they'll see it?" Jesse said.

"We'll put the oil lamp right in front of the window, to make it nice and bright. I'm sure they'll look at the house before they start. Now let's make some sandwiches, and then we'll go to bed. We can camp here in our sleeping bags."

A slamming door woke Carol in the gray dawn

light. She sat up in her sleeping bag and saw her parents looking down at her, still in their slickers.

"Mom, Dad!" She jumped up to hug them. "How did you get here?"

"The launch from the rescue station brought us over," Mom said. "They say our road should be dry by noon."

Carol looked out at the bay. It was no longer boiling, but just gray with whitecaps. The storm was over.

"We got your message, so we spent the night at the rescue station," Dad said.

Carol looked at the big window facing Cormorant Point and smiled. Taped on the glass in strokes big enough to read from a quarter mile away were the words she'd spelled out the night before: WE'RE OK.